Black Rose

God bless you!
Michaela Leigh

Black Rose

Michaela Leigh
Injoy, Inc.

Black Rose

Published by Injoy, Inc.
www.injoyinc.com
ISBN # 978-0-9794842-6-1

This book or parts thereof may not be reproduced in any form, stored in a retrieval system or transmitted in any form by any means – electronic, mechanical, photocopy, recording or otherwise – without prior written permission of the author, except as provided by United States of America copyright law.

Cover design by Laurel Popejoy of

Pure Image Photography and Graphics,
www.pureimagegraphics.com

Copyright © 2010 by Michaela Leigh
All rights reserved
Printed in the United States of America

Acknowledgments

I would like to thank my Aunt Shari for giving me the opportunity to fulfill a dream I've had for a very long time. To my mom, thank you for the countless hours that you've helped me on this project...you've no idea what that has meant to me. To Laurel, thanks for taking my ideas and using your imagination to make me a great cover! And lastly, to my mom, dad, Granny, Pa, Aunt Tara, Uncle Steve, and Minnie thank you for always encouraging me and believing in me.

Table of Contents

Chapter I..9
Chapter II...13
Chapter III..17
Chapter IV..21
Chapter V...27
Chapter VI..35
Chapter VII...43
Chapter VIII..49
Chapter IX..55
Chapter X...57
Chapter XI..61
Chapter XII...67
Chapter XIII..73
Chapter XIV..77
Chapter XV...85
Chapter XVI..89
Chapter XVII..95
Epilogue...97

Chapter I

The spring coastal wind made Agatha Moore pull her shawl tighter around her and wish she had worn the warm coat that still hung on a peg by the blazing fire at her home in Torquay, England, overlooking the North Sea. Agatha was an attractive, dark-haired young lady in her mid twenties, and only stood about five feet tall, but she was everything that was not expected of a young woman in 1914. She lived alone, was very independent, did not have a husband or even a beau, and had a full-time job.

Her job as a reporter at the local newspaper, *The Herald Express*, was at times very exciting, although it recently had become routine and mundane. As she quickly walked to the offices of *The Herald Express*, she thought about the events of the past week. Jack Tyler, one of her co-workers, had been acting strangely recently. One day when he had said that he was at home sick, Agatha had seen him walking into the library, even though a closed sign had been hanging in the window. It had seemed strange, but soon after that, things slid back into routine once again, and Agatha forgot about the peculiar sighting.

John Masters, looking forward to his upcoming wedding, had passed out invitations to everyone in the building. Even the cleaning crew had received invitations. Michael Mercer, the proof-reader, was busy packing and getting ready for his move to Washington to take a job with a larger newspaper. The office floor that Michael had worked on was throwing a surprise going-away party for him that week. Shawn and David Christie, the two handsome brothers, work from dawn to dusk as carpenters and reporters. People had begun to wonder whether they were full-time carpenters and part-time reporters, or vice versa. Melissa, the store keeper's daughter, was very kind and extremely shy, but she was slowly coming out of her shell. These few people made up the small social circle that Agatha called her friends.

Her family was even smaller than her social circle. Her two sisters were the only family she had. Her parents had been killed in a buggy accident. Ever since then, Agatha and her older sister, Mary, had tried to provide a good home and education for

Chapter I

their little sister, Alice. Mary had a part-time job as a seamstress at the general store in town. Her husband, Robert, was a surveyor and was constantly out of town working. Sarah, their little two-year-old, thought that Alice had been born to be her playmate. Mary and Robert had taken Alice in and raised her as their own.

As Agatha was on her way to the building where she constantly wrote columns on the latest local news, she decided to take a shortcut through an alley. She found herself wishing that something would happen to break up the monotony of work as of late. In the alley, the buildings were so tall that Agatha could not see the sun unless it was directly overhead. Walking further into the alleyway, Agatha could see a large heap on the ground ahead of her. As she got closer, she could see that the form on the ground was a man. The sun climbed higher into the sky and illuminated the swollen, blood-stained face of the man lying lifeless. Agatha immediately recognized him as her co-worker Jack Tyler.

Chapter II

At the constable's office, Agatha was thoroughly questioned about the murder of Jack Tyler.

"Did you see anything out of the ordinary, Miss Moore?" the constable asked in a deep monotone voice.

"Well, if seeing a dead body on my way to work is out of the ordinary, then yes, I did." replied Agatha sarcastically.

"Did you see anyone else besides Mr. Tyler in the alley?"

"No."

"That's all the questions I have for now. Just don't leave town." the constable said authoritatively.

"Now that you're finished questioning me, can I ask you a question?" Without waiting for a reply, she quickly continued. "What killed Jack Tyler?"

"He was beaten to death. He had several broken bones. One

of his broken ribs had punctured his heart and caused internal bleeding. The blood poured into his lungs causing him to drown." answered the constable.

When Agatha reached the newspaper office, she found on her desk a small note that read, "See me in my office immediately, Charles Brewster."

Mr. Brewster was the editor for *The Herald Express*. When Agatha entered Mr. Brewster's office, he asked her to sit down, which always meant that a long conversation was ahead of her.

"Agatha, you've been through a lot today. Go home, take a couple of days off."

"Go home? What would I do there? I can't just sit around reading or doing nothing for two days straight!"

"Well, you could knit some of those scarves with the pretty little flowers on them." Mr. Brewster said with a chuckle.

"I hate to knit, and I can't sew." Agatha retorted.

"All right, I'm not going to argue with you on this because the doctor says it's not good for my heart, but if you're going to work I want you to write an ongoing crime column keeping up with the latest on Jack Tyler's murder."

"Sir, if the constable knows anything, he's not sharing."

"You're too curious for your own good. Take a few days off, find out as much as you can, and write about it. Take this assignment and run with it. " replied Mr. Brewster.

"Thank you, sir!"

Chapter II

On her way back to her office, Agatha stopped and picked up the morning's newspaper. As she walked to her office, reading the newspaper as she went, she accidentally bumped into David Christie. David was a fellow part-time reporter, in his late twenties, who had dark hair, chocolate brown eyes, and stood a little over six feet tall.

"You're awfully late for a Monday. Is everything all right?" David asked in a deep and concerned voice.

"I'm just a little shaken by the dead body I found this morning on my way here. That's why I'm a little late."

Agatha quickly walked to her office to start taking notes for her column. David followed her into her office.

"Who died?" asked David with a puzzled yet concerned look on his face.

"Mr. Brewster didn't tell you?"

"Tell me what?"

"Jack Tyler was beaten to death last night, and I'm the one who found his body."

"Then why are you still here?"

"Why not?"

"Well, haven't you been through enough for one day?"

"Yes, but I don't want to go home and be alone. So, to keep my mind off what happened…I'll work."

"What are you working on?" David asked, walking around to the side of the desk where Agatha was seated.

"Mr. Brewster gave me a few days off to do some research on how Jack Tyler died."

"You're just nosey enough to find out who did it." David said with a slight grin.

"I'm not nosey. I just like to know what's going on. I'm inquisitive."

"Aggie," David said, using the nickname that he had made up for her, "That is being nosey."

"Well, either way, I'm going to find out what happened."

"How? Where will you even start? Nobody even knew Jack Tyler that well. He was a bit of a loner. " David replied.

"I know that. I don't need people to tell me what happened, I need events."

"He was pretty secretive. What kind of events do you think you need?" David questioned.

"The week that Jack said he was at home with the flu I saw him going into the library when it had a closed sign hanging in the window."

"You're not going to do what I think you're going to do, are you?"

"Yes! I'm going to break into the library!"

Chapter III

The next day, as Agatha made her way towards her office, she mentally planned a list of things she would need to break into the library. When she reached her office, newspaper in hand, she got out a sheet of paper and had begun writing out her list when Shawn walked in. He walked over to her desk and leaned over to read the first item on her list.

"Number one", he read, "A hammer? What are you going to do, rob a bank?"

"No," replied Agatha, "Did David say something to you?"

"No. Should he have?"

"No…not really. It's better that you don't know." Agatha said with a twinkle in her eye.

"All right, but if you and David are doing something illegal, please leave me out of it." said Shawn as he walked out of her office with a boyish grin on his face.

At the end of the day as Agatha stood on the sidewalk buttoning her coat and preparing herself for the long walk home, David strode up beside her.

"Need a ride?" he asked her.

"In what?"

"In my vehicle."

"You have a vehicle?"

"Yes. I bought it two months ago to haul supplies for my carpentry business."

"Well then, I would like a ride, thank you."

David placed his hand on the small of her back to guide her towards the parking lot. While gesturing with his other hand he said in a poor imitation of an American accent, "This way, Miss."

As Agatha stepped into the vehicle, in the same fake American accent David said, "Watch your step."

"Why, thank you, kind sir." said Agatha, playing along with the American tourist act.

"So, is tonight the big night?" David asked.

"Yes, tonight I go to the library."

"Do you have everything you need?"

"I think so. I have a list." she said, pulling the piece of paper out of her handbag.

"What do you think you will need?"

"Would you like to hear my list?" Without waiting for a

Chapter III

reply, she began reading. "Number one, hammer. Number two..."

Before she could finish reading the second item, David interrupted her. "Wait, wait. A hammer? Why on earth would you need a hammer?"

"I don't know, but I might need it for some reason."

"How long is this list of yours?"

"I have about seventeen things on my list."

"Seventeen! If you try to take all that with you while you're breaking into the library, you'll just end up getting caught."

"By the way you say that, I'm guessing that you have some suggestions for what I need."

"Yes. My first suggestion is, let me come with you."

"I don't need any help." protested Agatha.

"You don't even know what to take. And I bet you don't know how to pick a lock, either. Trust me, you need my help."

"I could use that hammer to pick the lock. Besides, do I even want to know how you got so knowledgeable about break-ins?"

"Meet me at the library tonight at eleven. Leave all seventeen of your 'necessities' at home, and I'll bring what's really needed." David said with a smile that lit up his entire face.

"Are you sure you want to get involved?"

David answered with a half grin, looking deep into her eyes,

"I was involved the minute I found out you were involved."

Chapter IV

That night, Agatha waited and waited in front of the library for David. Finally David came at ten minutes after eleven.

"Where were you? You're late." Agatha said, pointing at the large clock, on the front of the bank, across the street.

"Keep your voice down." David whispered, "Besides, according to my watch, I'm on time. The bank clock is fast."

"Or maybe your watch is slow. Either way, where is everything you said you would bring?"

"Right here!" David said, holding out his hands, which were empty.

"How are you going to tackle that lock with just your hands?"

"Do you have a hairpin?"

"Of course I have a hairpin. Why?"

"Just give me the hairpin, please."

"Oh, all right!" she said pulling a hairpin out of her hair. As she handed it to David, mounds of black hair tumbled down to her waist.

"Thanks." David said, looking into her eyes in a way that made Agatha blush and turn away.

Eventually, they picked the lock and entered the library prepared to snoop around.

"We probably ought to start looking around in Mr. Percy's office." whispered Agatha.

Samuel Percy, the librarian, was, like Jack Tyler, very secretive and somewhat reclusive. He practically lived at the library. Nobody even knew where he lived or where he went when he was not at the library. In Mr. Percy's office, wide shelves stretched from the floor to the ceiling. They were full of old classic books that could not be checked out. On the middle shelf, between an edition of *Pride and Prejudice* and *Romeo and Juliet*, sat a mysterious little box that had no lock but would not open.

"What are we looking for?" asked David.

"I don't know. Anything that seems different or out of place."

"Aggie, haven't you seen this place? Mr. Percy keeps everything in its proper place."

"Look at this box. It looks like it should open, but it doesn't have a keyhole."

"Let me see." he said, taking the tiny box from her hands and

Chapter IV

pressing in on its bottom.

"Don't break it!" Agatha gasped.

"But it's made to be broken." David said with the same boyish grin that his brother had.

As David stood there smiling at Agatha, trying to 'break' the box, the bottom of it suddenly slid back and part of the front slipped down revealing a keyhole.

"There's the keyhole." Agatha said, inspecting the box. "But where's the key?"

"Sometimes when someone wants to hide something, they'll separate the lock from the key. But a really smart person will keep the lock and the key together…just not in plain sight." As David studied and manipulated the box, the bottom of the box slid to the right and the left side slid forward, disclosing a small gold key.

"Would you like to do the honors?" David asked, holding up the small key in his large calloused hand.

"Why thank you, kind sir." Agatha replied, taking the key.

When they peered inside the box, they saw a small note and a pocket watch. The note read:

> *Dear Samuel,*
>
> *This pocket watch is your first clue to finding my emergency money. You're smart. I know that you can follow these*

> *clues to my inheritance. If anything happens to me, find the money and give it all to my wife. Until then, these clues must remain secret. If anyone were to find my father's vast fortune, it could mean murder.*
>
> *Sincerely,*
>
> *Jack Tyler*

"Vast fortune. Sounds like enough money to kill over." said Agatha.

"That's the only motive I can think of for Jack's murder." David said, picking up the pocket watch and beginning to inspect it.

As the lid popped open, the glass piece fell off. Inside the watch lid was a picture of a lemon.

"That's strange." whispered Agatha, as she picked up the glass piece off the floor. As she stood there inspecting it, she and David heard the sound of a key unlocking the front door.

"Oh, no! What do we do?" Agatha gasped.

Standing in the center of the windowless office, they realized it would be impossible to escape any other way except through the office door.

"Quick! Hide in the closet." David said, hurrying to put the box back together and shoving the note and the watch into his

Chapter IV

pocket. David quickly put the box back on the shelf and ran into the closet with Agatha. As soon as the closet door closed, the office door opened.

Samuel Percy entered the room and immediately walked over to the box and picked it up. He began trying to figure out how to open it. Eventually, the lid creaked open, and Mr. Percy realized the box was empty. He frantically searched for what may have been hidden in the box. He searched through every drawer, crack, and corner in the office, but found nothing. Then he realized that he had not searched the closet. As he slowly turned the handle, David pushed the door open with his shoulder, hitting Samuel in the head. Samuel fell to the floor unconscious.

"Don't worry, he will wake up soon enough. Now, let's get out of here!" David said grabbing Agatha's hand and pulling her out of the library. "We have about thirty minutes before he wakes up and notifies the constable. Where do you want to go?"

"The watch might have a clue about where we should go next." said Agatha, reaching into David's pocket and taking the watch.

As they studied the watch they noticed a small gold eagle engraved on the front of it.

"Wait, an eagle. That eagle is the symbol of the Warrior." Agatha said, as she pondered what this could mean and where they should go.

"Is that supposed to mean something?" asked David.

"Yes, there's a place called Warrior's Pub outside of town and it has an eagle just like this one on the sign."

"Then that's where we should go next!" David exclaimed.

Chapter V

Inside the Warrior's Pub, many men sat at tables drinking and talking loudly. At the back of the pub was a small desk, behind which sat a shelf with several slots in it. It was a miniature post office.

"Is there any mail for a Mr. Jack Tyler?" Agatha asked the man sitting at the desk.

"Yes, there is." the old man said, handing her a thick envelope.

"When did this letter arrive?"

"Sometime last week."

"About Tuesday, maybe?" asked Agatha

"Yeah, that's right." said the old man. "How'd you know that?"

"A lucky guess." Agatha thanked the postman and walked

back over to David, handing him the letter.

"The next clue?" asked David.

They walked outside and sat down on a bench in front of the old general store. Inside the letter, they found three blank pieces of paper and an old skeleton key.

"I wonder if the watch has something to do with this." said Agatha, as she picked up the watch. "I'll take it home with me tonight."

"I'll walk with you." said David, as he stood up and reached for Agatha's hand.

"No thanks, I can get home by myself."

"I don't mind. Besides, your house is on the way to mine."

"No it isn't."

"Minor detail." he said with a grin, reaching out once again to take her hand.

This time Agatha accepted, and while they walked towards her home they discussed the day's events.

"Do you think anyone besides Samuel and us knows about the box and watch?" asked Agatha, kicking a rock as they walked along.

"Do you think Samuel even knew that the watch was in the box?" replied David.

"But what if Jack told someone else about it?"

"By the way the letter was written, it seems that Jack wouldn't have told a single other person." David concluded.

Chapter V

"I guess you're right." Agatha said quietly.

"I'm sorry. What did you say?" David teased, cupping his hand around his ear.

"Fine," Agatha sighed. "I guess you're right."

"I was wondering if you'd ever realize that fact." he laughed.

As Agatha began to protest David's last remark, it began to rain.

"Run!" David said, grabbing Agatha's hand. They ran as fast as they could, and when they reached her house they paused on the covered porch.

"Well, it's been a lovely evening." said Agatha, laughing as she tried to brush the dust and rain from her skirt.

"I guess I'll be leaving now." David said with a smile, turning slowly to walk down the stairs.

As Agatha watched David walk down the stairs out into the rain, a flood of guilt swept over her and she found herself saying, "Wait!"

David turned around to look into her eyes. "Would you like to come in and sit a while until the rain lets up?"

"Don't mind if I do!" He grinned broadly and headed back up the steps two at a time.

"I'm going to dry off a bit. You can dry off over there." said Agatha, pointing towards a small room with towels and a washbasin.

After David had dried off, he looked around Agatha's neat

and orderly household. In the living room was a small shelf filled with classic first edition books standing at Agatha's height. As David stepped closer to the shelf, he fully realized how much taller he was than Agatha. The shelf came to about his shoulders. As he carefully looked over her books, Agatha walked up behind him.

"Are you admiring my books, or are you finally realizing how short I am?" asked Agatha with a little laugh.

"I was just looking at your books." David said as he turned around and gazed at Agatha with an expression that made her blush. "You look amazing." David placed a hand on the back of her head and smoothed her hair.

"Thank you. This was only clean dress I had. I haven't had a chance to do my laundry." Agatha felt her cheeks flush. She wondered why she had said that, because the truth was that she had an entire closet full of clean dresses. She had chosen her teal and black lace dress because her sisters had always said that it was her most flattering dress, and the teal made her eyes dance. Agatha questioned why she wanted to look her best for David.

"While you're here, would you like to go over the clues?" Agatha asked, holding up the watch and envelope.

"All right." he said, taking the items and setting them on the small table in front of the love seat.

When Agatha sat down she picked up the watch and popped

Chapter V

open the lid. Yet again, the glass piece fell out onto the floor.

"This annoying thing." said Agatha as she picked up the piece of glass from the floor.

"Maybe it's supposed to do that." mused David, taking the glass piece from her hand and looking at it intently.

"What do you mean?"

"It might show us something when it's out of the watch. It only shows the time when it's inside." David explained, holding up the glass piece.

"You mean what if the glass piece shows us something besides the time?" asked Agatha, as she took the glass piece from David and placed it back inside the lid of the watch. "Maybe it has something to do with this lemon on the inside of the lid."

As the glass piece slid into place, the picture of the lemon changed. The picture of the lemon was now poised over flames of fire.

"Lemon juice!" exclaimed Agatha.

"Is that supposed to mean something?"

"Of course it means something! It means that we need to put lemon juice on the three letters!"

"What about the flames?" asked David.

"Give me just a minute." Agatha said, as she dashed up the stairs.

A few minutes later, Agatha slowly walked back down the

stairs carrying a heavy clothes iron.

"What's this for?" David asked as he took the iron.

"We heat the iron in the fireplace, put some lemon juice on the blank pieces of paper, and then iron the paper."

"All right." David said in a questioning manner as he placed the iron in the fireplace.

"Where is the envelope?"

"It's right here." David said, pulling the envelope out of his chest pocket.

After they had squeezed the lemons and painted the juice on the pages, Agatha quickly ironed the pages, and the two began to read them. The first letter read:

> *Dearest Marissa,*
>
> *I know that I have never really expressed my feelings for you, but I hope that you knew and will always know that I loved you more than anything else in the world. I'm sorry that you thought I was keeping secrets from you. I kept only one thing from you, and that was the fortune I inherited from my father. I didn't tell you for your own good. If anyone else*

Chapter V

> *had heard about the money, it would have been far too dangerous for you. Trust me; it truly was for your own good. I have left clues for Samuel Percy, the librarian. He will find the money and give it to you. Please trust me; it is much safer for you this way.*
> *With all my love,*
> *Jack*

"Do you think his wife did it?" asked Agatha, folding up the letter and picking up the second one.

"I doubt it. The way the letter sounded, it seems that Jack and Samuel were the only people who knew about the money."

"Maybe Samuel decided to take the money for himself, and then turned on Jack and killed him." suggested Agatha.

"That sounds more believable than the wife." David chuckled.

"It's not that funny." said Agatha as she looked up at the mantel clock, "It's already three thirty!"

"I should go." David said, standing up and reaching for his still-wet coat slowly drying by the fire.

"But what about the other two letters?" Agatha asked, as she held up the two damp pieces of paper.

"Well, if you insist, I'll stay." he said with a broad grin, sitting down once again on the love seat next to Agatha.

Once David had sat down, he rested his arm on the back of the love seat around Agatha's shoulders. As they sat in silence, Agatha felt somewhat nervous with David's strong arm around her. Finally she decided that she should not have to feel uncomfortable in her own home, so she politely picked up David's hand and set it on his knee. As they sat close beside each other, neither saying a word, Agatha felt her eyelids growing heavier and heavier. She now realized just how tired she had become. Eventually the overwhelming urge to close her eyes overcame her, and she fell into a deep, peaceful sleep.

Chapter VI

The next morning when Agatha awoke to the sound of a loud rap on the door, she found herself curled up on the love seat next to David. Her hand gently rested on his chest as it repetitively rose and fell. The sounds of a key, and the door opening, jarred Agatha awake. There stood her two sisters, Mary and Alice. A gasp escaped Mary's lips as she put her hand over Alice's eyes.

"Alice, go outside." Mary said, her hand still covering Alice's eyes.

"Do I have to?"

"Yes! Go outside now!"

"What are you doing here?" asked Agatha as David began to wake up.

"It's Tuesday. Don't you remember? You were supposed to take Alice for some grown-up girl bonding time." said Mary, putting her hands on her hips.

"Oh, no! I completely forgot."

"Well, I see that you already have company, so I won't inconvenience you. I'll take Alice to work with me."

"But we didn't do anything wrong!" protested David.

"Let your Maker be the judge of that!" shouted Mary as she left, slamming the door behind her.

"Well, that was harsh." said David.

"That's Mary for you. But, don't worry, she's not a gossip."

"Why should I worry?" asked David.

"You wouldn't want to get a bad reputation, would you?"

"A bad reputation? How could I have a bad reputation if people said I spent the night with you?"

The awkward compliment brought color to Agatha's cheeks.

"You know where the washbasin is. I'm going upstairs to wash up." Agatha said as she started up the stairs.

Once in her small bedroom, Agatha opened the doors to her wardrobe. She stood indecisively, wondering which of her many dresses she should wear. She pulled dress after dress out of her wardrobe, but no dress was suitable: "This dress is too colorful. This dress doesn't have enough color." After much deliberation, she finally chose the perfect dress, a black and white pinstripe with a matching long-sleeve jacket. When she had buttoned the last button on the jacket, she gazed at herself in the mirror and sighed. "Well, I guess this will have to do."

It annoyed Agatha that suddenly she was concerned about her appearance and how David would think she looked. Agatha had

Chapter VI

always dressed stylishly, but had felt that to be too concerned with one's appearance and to become giddy over a guy was nonsense. So why did she find herself caring so much? After she had applied the finishing touch of a black hat to her ensemble and had neatly hung all her dresses back in the wardrobe, she descended the stairs.

As she neared the bottom of the staircase, she was greeted by the smell of fresh coffee. When she entered the kitchen, she found David sitting at the small kitchen table drinking coffee. A plate of eggs and bacon and a cup of coffee sat on the table across from him.

"Is this for me?" Agatha asked, pointing at the plate full of food.

"Who else would it be for?" asked David grinning boyishly.

"Thank you." said Agatha, before taking a bite of egg. "It actually tastes good."

"You seem surprised." said David, taking another sip of coffee.

They sat in silence, and Agatha's mind whirled with anticipation as she thought of what this new day would bring. *Would David stay around her all day? If he did stay, what would they do? Look for more clues?* As Agatha's mind raced, David broke the silence, interrupting her train of thought.

"I noticed that you pinned your hair back."

"Yeah?" Agatha inquired.

"Well…it…it still looks nice, of course…but…I…I like it down." David said, staring at his coffee cup and trying to avoid eye contact with Agatha.

"Thank you." Agatha said as she immediately felt her face flush. The funny thing was, she was almost certain that she had seen some red on David's cheeks as he sat staring at his coffee cup.

"So, what about those other letters?" David said, his dark chocolate eyes playfully dancing.

"They're right here." she said pulling the two remaining letters out of her jacket pocket.

"I'll get the lemons."

"And I'll get the iron." Agatha said, as she took her now empty breakfast plate towards the sink.

"No, I'll do that." said David, reaching to take the dirty dishes from her.

"I may not be able to cook and make food taste good, but I can clean up." said Agatha, smiling and tightening her grip on the plate.

"I know you can do it, but that doesn't mean you should have to." said David, looking down into Agatha's eyes and smiling that boyish grin that she was beginning to grow so fond of.

"All right," she said, releasing her grip on the dish, "but I get to dry."

Once his sleeves were rolled up, David started pushing and

Chapter VI

pulling the handle on the indoor water pump, which was not producing any water.

"Is this thing supposed to work, or is it a decoration?" asked David, still pushing and pulling on the handle.

"Oh, this thing...it never works." Agatha said, persistently trying to force water from the dry pump.

"Maybe it just needs a strong touch." David said, as he wrapped his arms around her. Placing his large hands on hers, he began pushing and pulling on the pump handle.

As Agatha stood there, trapped between David's strong arms, she hurriedly thought about her situation. David's large hands, tough and calloused, completely covered hers. Hands like that belonged to a hard worker. Though his hands were strong, they were also gentle. As they stood there repetitively pushing and pulling on the pump handle, the reality of the situation began to set in. Agatha could feel David's warm breath on the back of her neck. That made her feel somewhat uncomfortable, but it surprised Agatha more that David's strong arms surrounding her did not bother her. Finally, Agatha broke the silence. "Well, since no water is coming out, we should get the water from the pump outside."

"All right." said David, and the motion of the pump handle ceased, but he did not release his gentle grip on Agatha's hands.

After a moment, Agatha looked up at David with a questioning look, wondering why he had not let go of her hands.

As David looked into her eyes and began to lean towards her, Agatha's thoughts whirled in circles over what was about to happen.

Is this it? Is he really going to kiss me? But then a thought of propriety entered her mind. David had already spent the night at her house. A single girl who had no beau…to add a kiss to her list of 'wrong-doings' would not help matters much for her or for David. She quickly turned away, and David placed his disappointed kiss on her hat.

"We should probably read those letters." said Agatha, not wanting to make eye contact with David.

"That would probably be best." he said, releasing her hands.

"Forget the dishes. I'll do them later."

After they had painted the pages with lemon juice and ironed them, Agatha read the first letter aloud.

> Dear Samuel,
>
> I am sorry that it has to work out this way, but it could mean murder if anyone were to find these clues. As you know the three motives for murder are money, love, and covering up a crime. Your next clue is near our favorite fishing hole. Go there, and you will find your next clue close by.

Chapter VI

Jack

The second letter read:

> *Going for Water*
> *By Robert Frost*
> *To listen ere we dared to look*
> *And by the brook our woods were there*
> *But once within the wood, we paused*
> *To seek the brook if still it ran*
> *The barren boughs without the leaves*
> *Like pearls, and now a silver blade*

"What is it with people and poetry?" asked David.

"Well, poetry is how some people express their feelings and their emotions."

"Trust me, if I had feelings or emotions I wanted to express, I wouldn't need poetry to express them for me." said David, looking into Agatha's eyes and grinning quite boyishly. His bold statement made the color rise to Agatha's cheeks, and she promptly changed the subject.

"So…um…what about the key?"

"I don't know." David said, picking up the key and turning it in his large hand.

"Maybe we should go into town and talk to the librarian, ask him about the fishing hole."

"That's a good idea, but I still have to go to work. Do you need a ride?" asked David, as he slipped into his coat.

Chapter VI

"Sure. Just let me get all of these clues packed up." said Agatha, gathering the letters and key.

Once in the vehicle, David asked, "What do you think the poem has to do with the mystery?"

"I don't know. It seems that the clues we're finding have nothing to do with Jack Tyler's murder. They seem to be all about his father's money."

"Maybe the two things are linked together."

"What do you mean?" asked Agatha.

"Maybe somebody killed Jack to get to his inheritance."

"If so, the only way to find the murderer is to find the money." said Agatha, as the vehicle entered town.

"What's going on there?" asked David, pointing towards the library, in front of which was a crowd of people and two constable cars.

"I don't know, but I'm going to find out." declared Agatha, as she stepped out of the vehicle and headed towards the library and the nearest constable. "Excuse me… excuse me, sir…what's going on?"

"Samuel Percy is dead."

Chapter VII

"But how?" asked Agatha, bewildered by the sudden news.

"Listen, lady, I'm busy here…and even if I wasn't, I'm not allowed to disclose that information." the constable replied gruffly.

The constable's harsh words infuriated Agatha. She was about to retort when David stepped up behind her and asked, "What's going on?"

"Samuel Percy is dead, and this…this man won't tell me anything!"

"All right, you stay right here." said David, placing his hands on Agatha's shoulders and gently guiding her away. David returned to the constable and tapped him on the shoulder.

"Lady, I told you…" began the constable, not even looking in David's direction.

"Sir?"

"Oh…I'm sorry. I thought you were that woman standing

over there." the constable said, pointing at Agatha.

"Ah, well, you see, she's my wife, and she's always been a bit of a snoop. My name is David Christie. I'm a reporter for *The Herald Express*. If I knew all the facts on this case, I could write a column on it. And I guarantee that you will be mentioned in it, Officer…?"

"Matthew Harland's the name." answered the constable, patting his large middle.

"What happened here, Officer Harland?" asked David, taking a paper and pencil out of his coat pocket.

"Samuel Percy was found early this morning by Melissa Hargrave, a local storekeeper's daughter."

"When was he found?"

"Approximately 8:30."

"How did it happen?"

"The victim was stabbed in the heart."

"With what?" inquired David, slightly annoyed by the constable's vague descriptions of the murder.

"A knife. It's a very special kind of knife. It was made in 1887 and comes with a scabbard, but the scabbard is nowhere to be found. I carried a knife like it when I was in the war."

"Could I possibly see the knife?" asked David.

"Well…"

"I'll write a detailed column about it." David baited.

"All right, you can see the knife. It's inside the library."

Chapter VII

Once inside the library, David discreetly looked around the room. Everything seemed to be in its proper place. Everything was just as it had been the night before when he and Agatha had broken into the library. However, the small panel box that had contained the watch was nowhere in sight.

"There's the knife." said the constable, pointing towards a large knife with dried blood on the end lying on the desk.

"What does that say?" asked David, as he leaned over the desk to inspect an inscription on the blade of the knife.

"Oh, that. My knife had the same thing engraved on the blade. It says 'HOSPITAL CORPS, U. S. ARMY'. The scabbard matches the knife, and also says, 'WATERVLIET ARSENAL'.

"About how long is the blade?"

"Eleven to thirteen inches."

"What's that?" inquired David, pointing towards a strange mark in the wooden handle of the knife.

"That's just a chip in the wood. It's nothing of interest."

"Are you sure about that?"

"Of course I'm sure!" proclaimed the constable, placing a pair of thin-rimmed glasses on his large, round face.

"I'm telling you, that is not just a chip in the wood!" retorted David.

"And I'm telling you that it's nothing!" the constable said, as he leaned down to more closely inspect the mark in the handle.

"Oh, my word! It's initials!"

"Whose?"

"I don't know. It's the letters J and T."

"*J and T*, David thought. "Jack Tyler! That knife belonged to Jack Tyler!"

"Is that all?" asked the constable, obviously irritated by David's prying questions.

"Yes, I think that's everything. Thank you for your time, sir."

Coming out of the library, David quickly walked down the steps towards Agatha. As he approached, Agatha could see that David was holding a notebook.

"I got it." David said, placing the small notebook in Agatha's hand.

"How did you get him to tell you all this?" inquired Agatha, as she flipped through the notebook.

"That doesn't matter. Samuel Percy is dead, and he was probably the only one who could have made any sense of that silly poem."

"Possibly, but you need to go to work and I have some things that I need to do on my own." replied Agatha.

"Do you need me to drop you off somewhere?" David asked with a grin.

"No thanks. I can walk."

"Just because you can walk doesn't mean that you have to." David said with that same mischievous grin.

Chapter VII

"All right." replied Agatha with a slight smile.

"Where to?" asked David, opening the passenger door of the vehicle and helping her inside.

"The general store, please."

"Why do you want to go to the store?" asked David.

"Because Melissa, the storekeeper's daughter, found Samuel Percy's body."

"So you're going to talk to her about what she saw."

"Exactly!" Agatha said with a smile.

Chapter VIII

"Hi, Melissa." said Agatha as she walked through the front door of the general store.

"Hi, Agatha." said Melissa sadly.

"What's wrong?"

"Didn't you hear? Samuel Percy was killed this morning, and I found him."

"Are you all right? Why were you at the library this morning?" Agatha inquired.

"I needed to check out a book." Melissa said hesitantly.

"Is that really why you were there?"

"Why does it matter? Sam is dead, and nothing can change that!" shouted Melissa despairingly.

"Melissa…" said Agatha, placing a hand on Melissa's trembling shoulder, "Why were you at the library so early this morning?"

"I…I…" began Melissa as tears began to pour down her

cheeks, "I was there to see Sam. Every morning we would meet and go down by the river to talk."

"Why did you go all the way to the river just to talk?"

"Because no one would ever find us there."

"You loved him, didn't you?" Agatha asked.

"Yes, very much. We never met anywhere but at the river because people would think it improper for me to love a man eighteen years older than me." cried Melissa.

"Did you ever go fishing when you went down to the river?"

"What does that have to do with anything?" Melissa sniffed.

"Oh, nothing, really…I'm just curious. Guess it comes with being a reporter."

"We never went fishing, but when Sam would talk about his childhood, he said that he went fishing all the time as a little boy. He even took me to his favorite fishing hole about a month ago."

"Where is it?" Agatha asked, trying not to appear too desperate for an answer.

"River Derwent. Why?"

"No particular reason. I guess I'm just too curious for my own good. I've taken up enough of your time. You've had a rough morning, and I don't need to trouble you any further. If you need anything…just ask."

As Agatha was turning to leave, Melissa asked, "Why did you ask about the River Derwent? Are you wanting to go

Chapter VIII

fishing?"

"Um...does it matter if I want to go fishing?" Agatha hesitantly replied.

"No. I was just thinking that if you need a pole, we have some for sale." Melissa explained as she dried her tears on her apron.

"Oh, well, thank you. I'll keep that in mind. I really should be going. Melissa, I am so sorry. Take care."

As Agatha opened the door to leave, Melissa pressed, "By the way, who was that fine-looking gentleman that dropped you off?"

"Oh...David...he's just someone I work with at *The Herald Express*. Why?" Suddenly Agatha felt very uncomfortable being asked the questions instead of asking them herself.

"No reason. You two make a very nice-looking couple."

"We...we...actually, there is no we. We are just friends." Agatha stammered.

"Maybe I read too much into it, but the way he looked at you...it was like he saw no one else."

"You must have read too much into it. We're just friends." Agatha stated.

"Agatha, I know that look when I see it. Sam looked at me like that, and I know he loved me." Melissa said with a tear in her eye.

"Melissa, stop talking like that! We're just friends."

"Whatever you say."

"I really do need to get going." said Agatha with a smile, closing the door behind her.

As Agatha walked through the busy streets of Torquay, Melissa's words echoed in her mind. "The way he looked at you, it was like he saw no one else. Sam looked at me like that, and I know he loved me." Agatha wrestled with her thoughts. *There is no way that he loves me. We're just co-workers and good friends, but nothing more. But what if Melissa is right? What if David really does love me?* The thought both intrigued and slightly frightened her. What if David did love her? What would become of both their lives?

The sound of a paper boy yelling "Paper! Paper! Get your paper here!" abruptly broke into Agatha's thoughts.

"Would you like a paper, Miss?" the young boy asked.

"No, thank you, but I would like to know where I could rent a rowboat."

"If a boat is what you're wantin, Miss, then go down the road two blocks and turn left. The boat shop will be on your right."

"Thank you very much." said Agatha, giving the boy a coin.

After following the directions the young boy had given her, Agatha found herself at a large run-down building partially hidden by two taller brick buildings. When Agatha knocked on the door, a gruff voice called from inside the building saying, "We're closed!"

Chapter VIII

"But the sign says open!"

"Well, we're not!" said the gruff man, quickly opening the door and, turning around the old wooden sign to read "closed" in bright red letters, quickly slammed the door in Agatha's face.

"Well, you don't have to be so rude about it!" said Agatha, opening the door and peeking inside.

"I'm not being rude. I just don't serve customers after closing time, and I'm closed!"

"I don't care! I need a boat!" Agatha retorted.

"I'm not selling any boats."

"I don't want to buy a boat. I just need to rent one."

"Who's wanting it?" the man asked gruffly.

"Agatha Moore."

"You're the one who wrote the obituary for Jack Tyler, aren't you?"

"Yes, I am. Did you know Jack?"

"Know him! Of course I knew him. We were in the war together."

"Oh, well, then…by chance, do you know his wife?"

"Marissa? Of course I know her. In fact, I just saw her yesterday." the man said, growing a little nicer with each detail he told.

"Where could I find her?" inquired Agatha.

"She lives over there," said the man, crossing over to a window and pointing at a two story stone house down the street, "and she works at the bank."

"Thank you very much." said Agatha, as she headed for the door.

"What about your boat?"

"Oh, yes...my boat. I'll come back later for the boat." said Agatha with a twinkle in her eye.

Chapter IX

After walking the two blocks back to the busy part of town, Agatha headed towards *The Herald Express* offices to tell David of her findings. In David's private office, Agatha told him of her discovery.

"I'd better go talk to this Marissa." said Agatha.

"You probably shouldn't go alone."

"Oh, David, stop being such a big brother. I'll be fine."

"Did a big brother ever do this?" asked David as he placed his hand on the nape of Agatha's neck and gently pulled her towards him to tenderly kiss her round, full lips.

Agatha had imagined her first kiss, but she had always expected to hear music and see fireworks. Actually, all that she noticed was David's strong arms wrapped around her and the tenderness between David's lips and hers.

When the loving kiss had ended, Agatha said with a smile, "I think it's safe to say that no big brother ever did that."

"I still don't think you should go talk to Jack's wife alone." David said, placing his hands on her shoulders.

"Don't worry, I'll be fine. This woman just lost her husband. I think she will open up more to another woman."

"Maybe."

"Oh, and would you mind renting a rowboat and taking it down to the pier on the River Derwent? I'll meet you there." Agatha said as she headed towards the door of David's office.

"All right. River Derwent pier in one hour."

"Better make it an hour and a half. Marissa might have a lot to say."

Chapter X

As Agatha walked towards Marissa Tyler's house, all she could think about was David's kiss. It seemed as if the kiss was some sort of breakthrough for her, as Agatha had never felt this way about a man before. The fact of the matter was that she did not know what she truly felt for David. Agatha gently touched her lips, recalling the special kiss they had shared. It was so unexpected, so unpredictable, and yet so wonderful! But then, the sight of the Tyler house brought her thoughts back to the present task at hand.

Agatha rapped on the door with the brass door knocker. She heard shuffling sounds, and finally a maid with a serious expression on her face answered the door. "What do you want?"

"Hello, my name is Agatha Moore. I worked with Mrs. Tyler's husband at *The Herald Express*. I'd like to speak with her, please."

"Mrs. Tyler is not receiving any guests right now. Maybe

some other time." the maid said shortly, beginning to shut the door in Agatha's face.

"No, I don't think so. It's of great importance that I speak with Mrs. Tyler now." said Agatha, pushing the door open and stepping inside the warm home.

"How impertinent!" the maid snapped.

"It's all right, Elsa. Let her in."

Agatha looked in the direction of the voice. Sitting in a beautifully furnished room was a tastefully dressed woman reading a book.

"You must be Marissa Tyler?" Agatha asked the young woman, who appeared to be near her own age.

"Yes, and you are?"

"Agatha Moore. I worked with your husband at *The Herald Express*. May I offer my condolences, ma'am."

"Will you be needing anything else, Miss?" inquired the maid.

"No, Elsa, that will be all." replied Marissa. "I'm sorry about Elsa. She can be rather over-protective. Please, take a seat."

"Thank you." said Agatha as she sat down.

"I assume you are here to talk about my husband."

"Yes, I am."

"Well, what about him?"

"Do you know of anyone who may have wanted him dead?"

"No. Jack never told me much about his personal life."

Chapter X

"What do you mean, he didn't tell you much about his personal life? You were his wife. You *were* his personal life."

"I may have been his wife, but he never told me anything. I don't even know who he worked with."

"If you don't mind my saying so, you don't seem too upset about your husband's recent and rather violent death."

"Miss Moore, you must understand. Even though we were married, we were never close or even good friends. He had his life, and I have mine." Mrs. Tyler answered coldly.

"I think I have taken up enough of your time, but I'd like to ask you one more question before I go."

"What is it?" sighed Mrs. Tyler.

"Where were you the day your husband was killed?"

"I was home the entire day. I was sick and didn't go into work."

"Thank you for your time, Mrs. Tyler."

"Why have you asked me so many questions about my husband?"

"Why do you think?"

"Well, my husband was murdered, and you're asking me questions: I'm a suspect, am I not?"

"Yes, you are." Agatha studied Mrs. Tyler's reaction.

"You're welcome to ask any of my staff. The day my husband was killed, I was at home all day nursing a bad cold."

"Believe me I will be speaking with every member of your

household. Good day, Mrs. Tyler." said Agatha, walking out of the room.

Chapter XI

After speaking with all of Mrs. Tyler's staff, each of whom confirmed the woman's alibi, Agatha made her way towards the pier.

"What took you so long?" asked David, rising from the rock he had been sitting on.

"Have you ever questioned six people in one afternoon?"

"I can't say that I have. Are you ready to go for a little ride?" David asked, tapping the side of the boat and flashing his boyish grin.

"As ready as I'll ever be."

As the rowboat glided across the smooth waters of River Derwent, Agatha tried to concentrate on the beauty that surrounded her, but all she could think about was David.

What if Melissa is right? What if David really does love me? And our kiss…was it a pledge of love and affection, or just an overwhelming flood of emotions?

"So, Aggie, where is this so-called fortune?" David asked, breaking into Agatha's thoughts.

"I don't know. It might be here, but I doubt it."

"What do you think we're looking for?"

"I suppose something out of the ordinary." replied Agatha, gazing into the crystal-clear waters of the river.

As their boat slowly glided along, they stared into the smooth waters, searching for anything that did not belong.

Finally, Agatha saw something dark at the bottom of the river. "What is that?" she asked, pointing at the murky shadow beneath the surface.

"I'm guessing you want me to go find out for you, right?"

Well…I… yes, please." replied Agatha with a broad grin.

"All right." said David, peeling off his jacket and tie. "Hold these." he said, handing the two items to Agatha. Jumping into the cool water, David disappeared beneath the surface.

After a few moments, David resurfaced. "I found something!"

"What is it?"

"This!" David said, handing Agatha a small box with a tiny keyhole on the front.

Agatha studied the box intently. Then, realizing that David was still in the water, she asked, "Aren't you going to get back in the boat?"

"Aren't you going to give me a hand up?"

Chapter XI

"Oh, yes, I'm sorry." Agatha said, stretching her hand towards David.

As David took hold of Agatha's hand, he looked deep into her eyes, grinning his usual boyish grin. Before Agatha guessed what was happening, she found herself flying through the air and landing in the cool water.

"You are absolutely terrible! I can't believe you just did that!" exclaimed Agatha, splashing David in the face.

"That's just part of my charm. Come on, Aggie, we may be working, but there's nothing that says we can't have a little fun!" David said, grinning as he dowsed Agatha with another wave of water.

"All right, Mr. Prince Charming, now you're gonna get it!"

Agatha and David began their water war. They acted like children. Splashing and laughing, pushing each other under the water. After their war had ended, Agatha said with a laugh, "I'm starting to get cold. We should probably get out of this water."

"I'll go build a fire." David said, as he helped Agatha back into the boat.

"Whatever for? I'll be home soon."

"If you want to catch a cold because you got your feet wet, go ahead. I'm going to stay here and build a fire."

"All right, I'll stay and warm up for a few minutes."

As they sat warming themselves by the fire, all David wanted to do was hold Agatha in his arms for a minute, even a second.

But he knew that after their kiss earlier that afternoon, there was no way he could embrace her if she were to maintain her good reputation. As David sat by the fire pondering his feelings, Agatha interrupted his thoughts by taking the hairpins out of her damp hair. David smiled as he watched her pull out each of the hairpins that had secured her long black locks.

"What are you grinning about?" Agatha asked.

"Oh, nothing...we should probably take a look at that box." stammered David, handing Agatha the little box.

"I believe we already have the key for this." Agatha said, producing the skeleton key they had found with the letters.

"I hope this works." said David, moving closer to Agatha as she inserted the key into the keyhole.

"It had better work."

Slowly Agatha turned the key, and the lid popped open with a click. Lying in a pool of water inside the box was a sealed bottle, in which was another letter. Agatha picked up the bottle and removed the letter.

"Would you like to do the honors?" Agatha asked, as she handed the letter to David.

"Why, thank you, Miss."

David took the letter from Agatha. As he unfolded it, Agatha slid closer to him so she could read over his shoulder. Feeling Agatha so close to his side made David's heart skip a beat. All he wanted to do in that moment was just wrap his arms around her

Chapter XI

and hold her, but propriety dictated that he should not. As they studied the writing, they immediately recognized it as the same hand writing from Jack Tyler's other letters.

The letter read:

> *Love, Death, and the Flower*
> *Black Petals lay across the hay,*
> *Crimson pools around his feet,*
> *A mirror so that only he can see,*
> *Last words dying across his face.*
> *Stems and thorns within the hand,*
> *Tears fall,*
> *A story from her face,*
> *Only the wind will hear,*
> *Strangled cries,*
> *Last blood,*
> *Pooling at his feet.*

"Jack Tyler certainly did like poetry." said David, handing Agatha the letter.

"I suppose, but I can't make any sense out of these poems."

"Well, maybe we can figure it out tomorrow."

"Tomorrow? Why tomorrow? The night is still young!"

"As much as I would love to stay out here all night with you, I need to get you home."

"Oh, all right, but you'll come pick me up tomorrow so we can work on this poem, right?"

"You can count on it!" David said, grinning his boyish grin, while his dark eyes playfully danced with delight.

Chapter XII

The next morning, Agatha once again stood in front of her wardrobe. Just like the morning before, she indecisively wondered what she ought to wear. She finally decided on a beautiful green dress with a black jacket. As Agatha looked at all her hats lined up on a shelf, she thought about what David had shyly stated the day before. He liked her hair down, long and flowing. Turning from her display of hats, Agatha walked over to the vanity that stood in the corner. Looking in the mirror, Agatha thought for a moment, then slowly began taking the hairpins out of her hair. As her dark hair cascaded down her back, she heard a knock at the door. Looking out her bedroom window, Agatha could see David standing on the front porch.

"Oh, no! I'm not ready yet!" Agatha said to herself as she ran down the stairs, trying to smooth her hair. "But why should I care how David thinks I look?" Agatha mussed up her hair, then, sighing, smoothed it once again and answered the door with a smile.

"Ready to go, snoop?" David asked, grinning.

"Ready as always!"

As they walked side by side towards the River Derwent, David asked, "So, what do you think this new poem means?"

"I'm not sure. But I was thinking, the Chatsworth House is right on the shores of the River Derwent. Maybe something will turn up on the grounds there.

"All right, the Chatsworth House it is." David replied, offering Agatha his arm.

As Agatha took hold of David's muscular arm, she looked up into his eyes and smilingly said, "Thank you."

Built in the 1700's, the Chatsworth House was an old mansion nestled on the banks of the River Derwent. Generations of the Chatsworth family had lived there since its construction. Currently, Mr. Lawrence Chatsworth, his wife, and seven children resided at the mansion, although at the time the Chatsworth family was vacationing in France.

As David and Agatha wandered across the grounds of the Chatsworth House, Agatha looked at all of the beautiful flowers that reminded her of those that had been in her mother's garden.

"Those look different." David said, pointing towards a large bush full of black roses.

"Yes, aren't they beautiful? Most people think that a black rose means death, but it actually symbolizes mystery and

Chapter XII

intrigue. The blue rose is a symbol of mystery, as well.

"What does this one mean?" David asked as he pointed to a beautiful red rose bush.

"The red rose is the symbol for love." Agatha felt the color rise in her cheeks as she answered David's question.

As they continued walking through the gardens, Agatha explained the meanings of many of the different flowers they saw. Finally, David had to ask, "How do you know all of this?"

"When I was little, my mother always had a garden, and since I was home schooled, learning the names and meanings of all the different flowers in her garden was just one of the many lessons she taught me."

"That's amazing! I'm impressed that you still remember all that after so many years."

"Hey! It wasn't that many years ago!" Agatha said, playfully smacking David's arm.

"I'm just kidding!" David said with a smile. At that very moment, Agatha looked more beautiful to David than ever before. To him, the beauty of the flowers could not even begin to compare to that of Agatha. For a moment, he just stood there quietly looking at her. But then reality set in, and David recalled the reason they were standing in the garden. "I guess we should try to figure out the meaning of this poem."

"I suppose you're right."

They read and reread the poem until it finally dawned on

Agatha. "Wait a minute…I got it! The title…in the title is the word 'flower', and in the first line of the poem it talks about black petals."

"And?" David waited with anticipation.

"Whatever we're looking for is going to be buried under the black rose bush in the Chatsworth gardens!"

"Aggie, just two days ago I broke into the library. Now you're asking me to dig up something, which may turn out to be nothing, from a well-guarded mansion garden?"

"Well…yes! David, I just have this feeling that I'm right."

"Well, count me in!" David said with his usual boyish grin.

"Thank you! I think we should come back…"

"We? There is no we in this. If you come with me, you'll just slow me down. I'll come back tonight…alone."

"Thank you, David." Agatha said with a twinkle in her eye.

As David and Agatha walked towards Agatha's house, they talked about the possible murderers of Jack Tyler and Samuel Percy.

"Who do you think the killer is?" asked Agatha.

"I don't know. Everybody seems to be a suspect. For a while it looked like Samuel Percy, but now he's dead."

"Anyone dead is above suspicion." Agatha replied.

"Then there's the constable…he said he had a knife just like the one that was used to kill Samuel Percy."

"And the boatman. He knew Jack and Marissa Tyler, and

Chapter XII

also knew where they lived." Agatha added.

"The wife has a pretty solid alibi, so she can't be a suspect."

"Well I don't like her, and I'm not buying her alibi. I think she is involved."

"Just because she's rich, condescending, patronizing, and somewhat cold doesn't make her a psychotic killer."

"Maybe, but I don't trust her." Agatha declared, as she walked up the steps towards her porch.

"Well, I need to go home and plan my illegal acts for tonight." David laughed.

"I'm more than willing to go with you, if you'll let me."

"No offense, but you will just slow me down."

"I know, I know. See you tomorrow!" Agatha said with a smile.

David started down the steps, stopped, turned around, and looked into Agatha's eyes. "You looked really beautiful today with your hair down."

"Thank you." Agatha said as she felt the color rising to her fair cheeks.

"Well, I'll see you tomorrow. Good night!"

Chapter XIII

The next morning, after Agatha had tried on three different dresses with matching hats, she finally chose a wine-colored dress with small black buttons running from the neckline to the bottom hem of the dress. After yet more deliberation, Agatha decided to forgo wearing a hat and left her long, hair loose and flowing.

After getting her hair to look just so, Agatha took a pen and paper and went out to sit on the front porch. While waiting for David, she worked on her article about Jack Tyler. When the mantle clock struck one, Agatha began to wonder where David might be. After waiting a bit longer, Agatha decided to go into town and find out if anyone had seen David that morning. Once in town, Agatha went to *The Herald Express* office to see if David was there.

"Hey, Agatha! You look worried. What's wrong?" asked Shawn Christie, David's younger brother.

"I'm not sure. Have you seen David?"

"No, but I just got here. He might be around here somewhere."

"Thank you." Agatha said, walking towards David's private office. However, when she reached his office, she found the door was locked. Agatha's heart sank. She asked everyone at *The Herald Express* if they had seen David that morning, but nobody had. She then went to the construction site where David often worked in the afternoon. No one there had seen him since the day before.

"It's like he's fallen off the face of the earth." Agatha told Melissa as they sat in the general store.

"Oh, Agatha, you're just overreacting. I'm sure everything is fine."

"Melissa, I just have a feeling that something terrible has happened."

"Have you asked everyone he knows if they've seen him?"

"Yes, I've checked *The Herald Express*, the construction site where David works in the afternoons…nobody has seen him since yesterday."

"Agatha…have you checked any of the hospitals?"

"No…do…do you think I should?" Agatha stammered.

"That's up to you. But if you're right about something being wrong, David might be in a hospital. If he is, wouldn't you want to be there with him?"

Chapter XIII

"Yes…yes I would." Agatha said, sniffing as the unexpected tears blurring her vision trickled down her cheeks. Somehow David had worked his way into her heart and, for the first time, Agatha admitted to herself that she had fallen in love with David Christie.

Chapter XIV

After asking at two other hospitals in the area, Agatha trudged slowly down the road towards the last hospital in Torquay. She hoped and prayed with all her heart and soul that nothing bad had happened, but she could not shake the feeling that something terrible had. Now she was so afraid that she would never have the chance to tell David how she felt about him. The sight of the tall hospital building coming into view almost made Agatha faint. Her stomach tightened in knots as she thought of what may await her inside.

Agatha asked at the front desk if they had a patient by the name of David Christie, but they had no patients by that name. Agatha was then referred to a middle-aged woman with graying hair. Again, Agatha asked if they had a patient by the name of David Christie.

"Hold on just a minute." the gray-haired lady said with a smile as she stepped into a small room and closed the door behind her.

A few minutes later, the woman returned and said, "We have no patients by that name, but we do have four patients that have not yet been identified.

"When did they come in?"

"Well…" said the woman, flipping through some papers in her hand, "two of the patients were admitted last week, and the other two came in last night."

"Could I please see the two who came in last night?"

"All right, follow me." the woman said with another sympathetic smile.

As they walked down the hallway, the smell of medicines made Agatha light-headed. The woman led Agatha into a small white-washed room with one large window, curtain drawn, in the corner. The room was so dimly lit that Agatha could not distinguish the face of the person lying in the hospital bed.

"I'll open the curtains for you." the woman offered.

As the woman drew back the curtains, sunlight slowly streamed through the window, illuminating the small room and the man lying still on the bed in the center of the room.

"No!" gasped Agatha. "That… that's David!"

"I'll leave you alone with him." the woman said quietly, turning and leaving the room.

"Oh, David, what happened to you?" Agatha cried, brushing his dark hair away from his forehead. No reply came from

Chapter XIV

David's pale lips. His strong, muscular arms lay limp on his methodically rising and falling chest.

A shuffling sound from behind made Agatha turn to see who was there. A man in a white coat smiled sympathetically. "Hello, I'm Dr. Bridges."

"Agatha Moore." Agatha said, shaking the doctor's hand. "What's wrong with David?"

"He was found last night at the Saint Morgenstern Church by a young couple there to be married. He sustained three gunshot wounds: one in the left arm, one in the right leg, and one in the chest. He's lost a lot of blood. That's why he's unconscious. Right now, what we truly need is someone who can donate blood."

"I'll do it!"

"Thank you for offering, but it works better if we directly transfer blood from one man to another."

Agatha fought back her tears, "Do you know who did this?"

"No, I don't. I'm sorry."

"Thank you, doctor."

After the doctor had left the room, Agatha returned to David's side. "Everything's going to be all right. Just please… please don't leave me now…please." begged Agatha, holding David's hand and gazing at him through a flood of tears.

Once again, Agatha heard a shuffle behind her. There stood the gray-haired woman. "I'm sorry, Miss, but you'll have to leave for now. We need to change his bandages."

"All right." said Agatha, rising and brushing away her tears.

"It will only be a few moments, and you can come back then and sit with him, if you'd like."

Agatha's throat tightened. She tried to speak, but the words would not come. All she could do was nod her head.

Agatha walked down the hospital hallway and asked a nurse where she could find a phone. Agatha hurried to the phone and called David's brother, Shawn.

"Shawn, I...I found David. I'm at Mercy's Brink Hospital. He's...he's been shot and needs blood. I would donate, but the doctor says it needs to come from another man." Agatha stammered and sniffed.

"I'll be there as soon as I can!"

After waiting for what felt like a lifetime but was just ten minutes, the gray-haired nurse told Agatha that she could go in and see David. As Agatha sat in the small hospital room, holding David's limp hand, she remembered the kiss they had shared. She had never told David what that kiss had meant to her, or how much he meant to her. Now she was frightened that she may never even get the chance to tell him that she loved him and...Shawn suddenly walked in.

"Oh, Shawn! I'm so glad you're here." Agatha said as she hugged him.

"How is he?"

Chapter XIV

"The same." Agatha could not fight back her tears any longer. She had tried to be strong, but this was just too much.

"Agatha, you look terrible."

"I'm fine."

"No, you're not! You need to lie down and get some rest."

"I'm not leaving him, and that's that!"

When another bed had been set up in the room, Shawn lay down while the doctor retrieved a long rubber tube with a long needle on each end. The doctor inserted one needle in a vein in David's arm and the other in Shawn's. Finally, blood began to run from Shawn's arm through the rubber tube into David.

After the blood transfer had been completed, the doctor and nurses left the room, leaving Agatha and Shawn alone with David.

"Some of the color seems to be coming back to his cheeks." Agatha said hopefully.

"Maybe a little. Agatha, do you know who did this to him?"

"All I know is that a young couple wanting to get married found him at Saint Morgenstern Church last night."

"If I ever find out who did this, I'm gonna kill him." Shawn said, quickly standing up.

"No, Shawn! I know you're angry and I'm angry, too, but please don't do anything you'll regret later."

"I'm going outside. I'll be back later." he said in a low tone, hurrying out of the room.

Two hours slowly ticked by, and Shawn had still not returned. Beginning to worry about what Shawn might be doing, Agatha decided to walk around the hospital. When she stepped out the hospital's front doors, she saw Shawn leaning against the brick wall smoking a cigarette.

"I didn't know you smoked." said Agatha, walking up beside Shawn and leaning against the brick wall.

"Neither did I." he chuckled mirthlessly, throwing the cigarette on the ground and grinding it with his heel.

"You didn't mean what you said earlier, did you?"

"I don't know what I meant."

"But you threatened to kill someone!"

"And I have good reason to!"

"There is never a good reason for taking someone's life."

"Agatha, please, just let me take care of my own business."

"Fine. I can see there's no reasoning with you, but I just hope you don't do something that you will regret." said Agatha, before going back into the hospital.

Back in David's hospital room, Agatha peered out the window and saw that Shawn's vehicle was no longer in the parking lot. She wondered if he had gone to find the person who had shot David. Staring at David's muscular form lying on the bed so helpless and weak, part of her hoped that Shawn would find the person who had put the three bullets in David. Then Agatha recalled the Biblical teachings that she had learned as a

Chapter XIV

child. *Thou shall not kill...vengeance is mine, sayeth the Lord.* Agatha knew in her heart that taking someone's life was a terrible thing to do.

Agatha turned her focus back to David. Making sure he was comfortable and praying was all she could do now. Kneeling beside David's bed, Agatha began to pray. "God, please don't let David die...please. I love him, and I don't think I could bear it if he died. Please, God, he's a good man, let this child of Yours' live. In Jesus name I pray. Amen."

Chapter XV

The sun had set, and the gas lamps had been lit to illuminate the darkened hospital rooms. Shawn had still not returned, and David had not awakened. Agatha sat silently in a chair beside David's bed, watching his chest rising and falling, praying that he would wake up so she could tell him she loved him. Occasionally, doctors and nurses came in to check David's pulse or to change his bandages, but, there had been no change in his condition. Rising, Agatha paced back and forth beside David's bed. The waiting was almost unbearable.

Once again, Agatha sat down in the chair beside David's bed and grasped his hand. "David...David, if you can hear me... you...you need to know...I've never loved anyone besides my family...until now. David, I love you...and I don't know if I could...if I could take it if you died. Please, David, please don't give up...you have to fight...you have to. Come back to me, David, come back." Agatha wept as she laid her head on David's bed.

Suddenly, Agatha felt someone's hand gently stroking the back of her hair. Lifting her head expecting to see a doctor or nurse or perhaps Shawn, she found David's dark eyes staring back at her above the weak smile on his face.

"David! You're alive!" Agatha cried. All senses of propriety left her, and she planted a loving kiss on David's lips.

When their kiss had ended, David chuckled quietly. "Now that's the way to welcome a man back to consciousness!"

"I was afraid you would die."

"What happened? Where am I?"

"You're at Mercy's Brink Hospital. You were shot three times and found at Saint Morgenstern Church."

"Now I remember. I went to the church to look for another clue."

"Do you know who shot you?"

"No. One minute I was reading the letter that I found under the rosebush, and the next I was laying on the floor of the church."

"Oh, David, I'm just so happy you're alive!"

"Me, too." David said, smiling weakly.

"I had better tell the doctor you're awake!" said Agatha, heading towards the door.

"Hey, Aggie."

"Yeah?" answered Agatha, turning back around to face

Chapter XV

David.

"I love you, too."

A smile lit up Agatha's face, and tears of joy streamed down her cheeks. Unable to resist the temptation, Agatha ran to him as quickly as she could and placed a kiss on his lips. With David's good arm wrapped about her, Agatha felt as though she could stay there forever.

Chapter XVI

A week had passed since David had awakened. He grew stronger by the day, and was becoming a terrible patient. David hated being treated like an invalid. Shawn had returned the day after David had awakened, and was finally beginning to act like himself again. He had not carried out the promised task of tracking down and killing the person who had shot David.

Since David was recovering, Agatha decided to leave him in the care of the nurses and visit Saint Morgenstern's Church to look for Jack Tyler's inheritance or another clue. Once inside the church, Agatha made a thorough search of every room, but found nothing out of the ordinary.

The note that David had found under the black rose bush had simply read "Saint Morgenstern's #5". The "number five" did not make sense. Agatha had hoped to find something with a five on it in the church, but, again, she found nothing. Next, Agatha went outside to look around. Behind the church there was a storm shelter, and when Agatha tried the door, she found it unlocked. After climbing down the creaky stairs, it took Agatha's eyes a moment to adjust to the darkness of the small room. Against the dirt walls stood a row of thirteen safes with numbers inscribed on top. After finding the fifth safe, Agatha remembered the "Going for Water" poem that had not made any sense. Among Agatha's own collection of books was a book of poetry that contained the same poem, so she knew it well. After reading Jack's letter, she had realized that Jack had not written the entire poem, merely portions. Agatha had copied the poem, thinking it might be useful at some point. Taking Jack's partial poem and her copy of the entire poem out of her jacket pocket, Agatha read and reread the lines.

"It finally makes sense!" Agatha said to herself. "Each line is from a section of the poem." Reciting the poem quietly, Agatha began numbering the lines and sections of the poem.

Finally, she had the lines and sections of the poem numbered. It was time to test her theory and to see if she had figured out the combination to safe number five.

Five…two…four…one…three…six. Agatha heard the safe click, and the heavy metal door creaked as she pulled it open. Lifting a burlap bag out of the safe, Agatha tried to open the bag, her hands trembling with excitement. Inside the burlap bag, lay several bundles of paper bills.

Suddenly, a man's voice from behind her said, "I'll take that,

Chapter XVI

if you don't mind."

Agatha whirled around and found herself trapped by two people, one of whom was a man pointing a gun at her. The man she did not recognize, but the second person was Marissa Tyler.

"You already know me, but this darling man is Ian, Jack's younger brother." Marissa said with a short laugh.

"Why are you doing this?" Agatha questioned.

"You see, Jack's father believed that his first-born son should inherit his vast fortune, but poor Ian would get nothing. When Jack's father died, his entire fortune went to Jack. To make matters worse, Jack believed in saving for that rainy day. He hid the entire fortune, and wouldn't tell anyone where it was because he was so paranoid about it. He just left those stupid clues for Mr. Percy, but you were clever enough to figure those out. For that, we thank you. You've made it possible for me to live in comfort with Ian, the man I truly love."

"In other words, we did all the work for you."

"Of course. And now that we have the money, I don't think we'll be needing your assistance any longer." Ian said, raising the gun towards Agatha's head.

Just then a shot rang out and Ian fell to the ground.

Looking up to the entrance of the storm shelter, Agatha saw Shawn standing in the doorway lowering a gun. Agatha hurried and picked up the gun that Ian had dropped when he fell to the ground.

"What are you doing here?" Agatha asked Shawn.

"David figured that, since he's feeling better, you'd come back to the church and try to figure out the next clue. And since he couldn't keep an eye on you, I said I would."

"Did you kill him?" Agatha asked, looking at Ian lying on the ground.

"No, I just wanted to give him a small taste of what David had to go through. He'll live." said Shawn, yanking the man to his feet.

Marissa and Ian were sent to prison on charges of second degree murder, and the money, that Jack had so carefully hidden was given to Saint Morgenstern Church. No one ever knew for sure why there were thirteen combination safes in the storm shelter of the church, but it was suspected that it had something to do with the Boer War that had been fought from 1899-1902.

Agatha turned in her piece to her editor, Charles Brewster, who printed the article on the front page of *The Herald Express*. David's injuries were healing nicely, and after just two months of recuperating, the only visible sign of injury was a slight limp, in David's right leg, which the doctor had said would heal within a few more months.

Two months later on a Friday evening, David invited Agatha over for dinner. Usually when Agatha went over for dinner, David would meet her and walk with her at least part of the way to his house…but not tonight. When Agatha entered his living

Chapter XVI

room, she immediately noticed several vases filled with blue, red, and black roses.

"What's all this for?" Agatha asked David as he entered the room.

"Oh, just something I've been planning for quite a while." David said, walking over to Agatha. Kneeling on one knee, David took Agatha's hands and said, "You mystify and intrigue me, and I'm desperately in love with you. Agatha Moore, will you marry me?" David held up a small black box in which lay a beautiful black diamond ring.

"Yes, yes, I will marry you!"

David stood up, and took Agatha in his arms, and passionately kissed her. From that moment on, everything else was a blur. All Agatha noticed was David's strong arms surrounding her, and the loving passion from the kiss they shared.

Chapter XVII

David and Agatha were married on Christmas Eve, 1914. Their wedding was a glorious occasion. Family and friends gathered as David and Agatha shared their first dance and kiss as husband and wife.

"Well, Aggie, I'd say you're worth getting shot for." David laughed as the couple walked hand in hand through the crowded reception.

"I'd hope so. You know, I used to hate the name Aggie, but now I rather like the sound of it, Mr. Christie."

"I'm glad, Mrs. Christie, because you'll always be my Aggie." David said, kissing the back of her hand.

"I think I also kind of like this mystery business. Maybe I'll write a mystery novel some day…but I doubt it."

Epilogue

The real Agatha Christie was born on September 15, 1890 in Torquay, Devon, England. Considered one of the greatest authors of all time, Agatha Christie wrote a grand total of ninety-one novels. She wrote eighty-seven novels as Agatha Christie, six as Mary Westmacott, and seven as Christie Mallowan, along with one autobiography.

Agatha's first novel, *A Mysterious Affair at Styles*, was published in 1920. Her novels have sold approximately four billion copies. Only the Bible has sold more copies than the Agatha Christie novels.

Agatha Mary Clarissa Miller was twenty-four years old when she married Archibald Christie on December 24, 1914. In 1919, at the age of twenty-eight, she gave birth to their only child, Rosalind. Agatha Christie died on January 12, 1976. She was 85 years old.